The Buried Biscuits

DARREL & SALLY ODGERS

Kane/Miller
BOOK PUBLISHERS

JACK RUSSELL: Dog Detective

Book #1 DOG DEN MYSTERY

Book #2 THE PHANTOM MUDDER

Book #3 THE MUGGED PUG

Book #4 THE LYING POSTMAN

Book #5 THE AWFUL PAWFUL

Book #6 THE SAUSAGE SITUATION

Book #7 THE BURIED BISCUITS

First American Edition 2008
by Kane/Miller Book Publishers, Inc.
La Jolla, California

First published by Scholastic Press in 2007
Text copyright © Sally and Darrel Odgers, 2007
Cover copyright © Lake Shore Graphics, 2007
Dog, Frisbee, courtesy of the Cansick family
Illustrations copyright © Scholastic Australia, 2007
Illustrations by Janine Dawson

Library of Congress Control Number: 2007932527
Printed and bound in China
1 2 3 4 5 6 7 8 9 10

ISBN: 978-1-933605-77-7

Dear Readers,

The story you're about
to read is about me and my
friends, and how we solved
The Case of the Buried Biscuits. To
save time, I'll introduce us all to you
now. Of course, if you know us already,
you can trot off to Chapter One.

I am Jack Russell, Dog Detective. I
live with my landlord, Sarge, in
Doggeroo. Sarge detects human-type
crimes. I have the important job of
detecting crimes that deal with dogs.
I'm a Jack Russell terrier, so I am
dogged and intelligent.

Next door to Sarge and me live
Auntie Tidge and Foxie. Auntie Tidge
is lovely. She has biscuits. Foxie is not
lovely. He's a fox terrier (more or less).

He used to be a street dog, and a thief, but he's reformed now. Auntie Tidge has even gotten rid of his fleas. Foxie sometimes helps me with my cases.

Uptown Lord Setter (Lord Red for short) lives in Uptown House with Caterina Smith. Lord Red means well, but he isn't very bright.

We have other friends and acquaintances in Doggeroo. These include Polly the dachshund, Jill Russell, the Squekes, Ralf Boxer and Shuffle the pug. Then there's Fat Molly Cat from the library.

That's all you need to know, so let's get on with Chapter One.

Yours doggedly,

Jack Russell – the detective with a nose for crime.

Fog Fight

The Case of the Buried Biscuits
began early one morning. First, there
was the fight with Foxie. Then there
were the boys, and the burrows in
the park. But I'd better start at the
beginning.

There was a thick white fog that
morning. I climbed out of my basket,
and sniff-sniffed down the steps. I
trotted across the lawn and did what
dogs do. Then I made a quick **nose
map**.

Jack's map:

1. My dinner bowl.

2. The knuckle bone Auntie Tidge gave
   me on Thursday.

3. Boys.

4. Rabbits in the park.

5. Fat Molly Cat, stalking a bird.

6. Unspecial biscuits.

It was time to plan my day. The knuckle bone was picked clean, but boys had sticks to throw. Sticks need someone to catch them. I could hunt rabbits in the park with Polly Smote. **Pawhaps** I might **terrier-ize** Fat Molly.

On the other paw, Foxie and I had done that on Friday.

I might visit Jill Russell down at the station. I hadn't seen her for a while. Or how about a **Jack-snack**? I sniff-sniffed again. Biscuits. Auntie

Tidge gave me **special biscuits**, but these smelled like the unspecial kind. I detected icing and jam. Maybe Sarge had put one out for me as a surprise? I checked my bowl. No biscuits. Maybe Foxie had some? I decided to pay my best pal a visit.

I got into Foxie's yard (never mind how). I checked his bowl, but it was empty.

The boys passed by on the other side of the fence. A bird twittered. Foxie snored. If there *were* biscuits around he hadn't noticed. I began to **pawtrol** the **pawrimeter**.

Again I whiffed biscuits. I **jack-yapped** to explain I wanted some. The boys took off at a run, and I heard a soft thud as something landed in Auntie Tidge's herb garden.

I was sniffing for clues when something bit the back of my neck.

"Gotcha!" snarled a voice.

Jacks are nimble, Jacks are quick. Jacks are always ready for a scrap. I tugged free, and snapped my **jack-jaws** around a hairy leg. Someone yelped. Sharp teeth closed on my tail. I yelped. Teeth clashed, ears flapped. The herbs smelled squashed, especially the garlic. I snarled.

"Jack! Cut that out! *Jack!*"

Sarge was calling, but a Jack on a mission never gets distracted. My mission was winning this scrap.

"*Jack!*" Sarge sounded cross.

"Foxie Woxie! Is someone hurting you?" That was Auntie Tidge.

Splooooosh! That was a bucket of cold water landing on my back.

I spluttered. So did my **oppawnent**. He snarled. "I'll get you for this, Jack Russell!"

I snarled back. "You and whose army, Foxie?"

"Me, my teeth and I!" My oppawnent nastily nipped my nose.

I yelped, and **jack-jumped** onto his back, snapping my fangs.

"Jack! Leave Foxie alone!" Sarge loomed out of the fog and grabbed my collar. Then he picked me up and carried me back to my yard.

<u>Jack's Facts</u>

If a Jack is attacked, humans come to the rescue.
They always turn up when the Jack has the upper paw.
Then they blame the Jack for the attack.
This is a fact.

Behind me, I heard Auntie Tidge arguing with Foxie. "No, Foxie, stop it. Put that nasty thing down. You can't have it."

Jack's Glossary

Nose map. *Way of storing information collected by the nose.*

Unspecial biscuits. *The kind of biscuits people eat. (Some people call them cookies.)*

Pawhaps. *Perhaps.*

Terrier-ize. *Frighten.*

Jack-snack. *A snack for a Jack.*

Special biscuits. *Auntie Tidge makes these. They don't harm terrier teeth.*

Pawtrol. *Patrol, done by a dog.*

Pawrimeter. *The outside of a dog's terrier-tory.*

Jack-yap. *A loud, piercing yap made by a Jack Russell terrier.*

Jack-jaws. *The splendid set of jaws owned by a Jack Russell.*

Oppawnent. *An opponent, a dog you happen to be fighting.*

Jack-jump. *A very athletic spring done by a Jack Russell.*

At the Shop

The fog had gone by lunchtime, but
Foxie was still angry. He wouldn't tell
me what Auntie Tidge had taken away
from him.

"Unfair! Unfair!" he yapped from
the other side of the hedge. "A dog has
a right to defend his **terrier-tory!**"

"A dog has a right to visit his pal,"
I snarled.

"A decent dog doesn't enter
without **pawmission!**" snapped Foxie.

"**Pawlite** dogs don't snore when a
pal visits!" I growled.

"Foxie Woxie? Stop it!" That was

Auntie Tidge.

Sarge came out and clipped on my leash. It was time for our Saturday walk.

I leaned towards the park, but Sarge said we had to go shopping.

I leaned harder, and muttered, "*Rrrrrrrrrr,*" to show what I thought of shopping.

"Don't you growl at me, Jack," said Sarge.

Jack's Facts

Bad dogs growl at their people. Grrrrrrr.
Good dogs sometimes mutter at their people. Rrrrrrr.
Muttering is not the same thing as growling.
This is a fact.

On the way to Tina Boxer's shop, I sniffed the air. I smelled Fat Molly and my knuckle bone, but no more biscuits.

I tried to put the morning out of my mind.

At Dora Barkins' house, the three Squekes yaffled in their yard, doing what Squekes do.

"We've been down to the park," they yaffled. "We saw rabbits. We saw boys. We chased sticks. We saw burrows. We…"

"Hurry up, Jack," interrupted Sarge. He was still cranky with me.

At the library, Fat Molly Cat was sunning herself on the steps. *"Yow-sptttt!"* she spat. I don't speak Cat, but I know swearing when I hear it.

I muttered at her, "*Rrrrrrrrrr,*" and
Molly spat again.

"Jack!" Sarge tugged my leash.

At Tina Boxer's shop, Sarge
clipped my leash to the rail. "Stay
there, Jack," he ordered. The shop bell
tinkled as he went inside. I heard Ralf
Boxer yap behind the shop.

<u>*Jack's Facts*</u>

People say "stay" when they tie a dog to a rail.
Dogs tied to rails have no choice but to stay.
*People are sometimes **im-paw-sible**.*
This is a fact.

The bell tinkled again. A woman came out of the shop. I sniff-sniffed the air and detected lamb chops and bread. She hadn't bought biscuits.

Walter Barkly came out with a bulging shopping bag. I sniff-sniffed the air. Walter Barkly had bought a roast chicken.

Gloria Smote tied Polly to the rail beside me. I sneezed and **snortled**.

Polly smelled of Pooch Polish.

Polly jabbed me with her sharp dachshund nose. "I went to see Jill Russell. I bet you didn't. Jill Russell has a secret."

Gloria Smote came out. She had bought more Pooch Polish.

Clack-clock-tonk. Spanggg! Clack-clock-tonk. Spanggg! Two boys were coming toward the shop. One had more freckles on his face than a Dalmatian. He was kicking a can. The other ran a stick along the fence. *Clack-clock-tonk. Clack-clock-tonk.* I pricked up my ears. These smelled like the boys who had passed my terrier-tory that morning. Was that a whiff of biscuit?

Kick stopped kicking, and stared

at me. "That's Sergeant Russell's dog. We'd better go." He and Stick turned and scooted away.

Jack's Glossary

Terrier-tory. *A territory belonging to a terrier.*

Pawmission. *Permission, given by a dog.*

Pawlite. *Polite, for dogs.*

Im-paw-sible. *Like impossible.*

Snortled. *A snuffle and a snort, caused by proximity to soap.*

 Biscuit Mystery

When we got home, I checked on
Foxie.

Foxie lifted his lip. He was still
angry, but he was ready to talk. "Auntie
Tidge is cross with me," he complained.
"Auntie Tidge blamed me for the
biscuits you put in her herb bed. She
took the biscuits away."

"I didn't put biscuits in her herb
bed. Those boys threw them over the
fence this morning."

Foxie snarled. "I didn't see any boys."

"You were snoring."

"What boys would throw away biscuits?"

Foxie had a point. I trotted past him and peered at the herb bed. There wasn't much to see, except squashed herbs. The smell made my nose itch.

"The biscuits are gone," said Foxie. "I told you, Auntie Tidge took them."

I sniff-sniffed anyway. Paw prints (mine), more paw prints (Foxie's), some shoe marks (Sarge's and Auntie Tidge's). There was still a faint scent of boy, mixed up with a whiff of biscuit. Was that chocolate? Then I saw a twist of shiny paper. I sniff-sniffed hard. Carefully, I gathered the evidence in my teeth.

"What have you got there?" Foxie was bouncing around, trying to see it.

"Careful," I mumbled around the
evidence. "You'll contaminate the
scene."

"That's chocolate paper," snapped
Foxie. He tried to grab it out of my
mouth. "Auntie Tidge has left it for me
to lick."

I spat out the evidence and
anchored it with my paw. "Don't be
silly, Foxie," I said. "This came from
those boys too."

"It's on my terrier-tory," growled Foxie. "That chocolate paper is rightfully mine."

I pawed the paper over and sniff-sniffed the other side. Had Stick or Kick touched this paper? If so, what did it mean? Before I could be sure, the paper had vanished. So had Foxie.

It was no use chasing Foxie and the chocolate paper, so I investigated the spot where it had been. I didn't learn much. The scent of chocolate and biscuit and boy was there, but the smell of herbs was stronger.

I went to visit Auntie Tidge. I did the paw thing, to show her I needed to investigate the biscuits.

"Hello, **Jackie Wackie**," she said. Then she picked me up and carried me home. "You stay here. Foxie is in disgrace. He's been stealing again."

Auntie Tidge was wrong, but I couldn't tell her. If I couldn't investigate the biscuits, I should investigate the boys.

The Squekes had seen boys at the park. Were they the same ones? Had they thrown a package of biscuits to the Squekes? I decided to **interrier-gate** the Squekes and find out.

I left my yard (never mind how) and trotted to Dora Barkins' place. The Squekes were in the yard, **jaw-dueling**.

"Stop, in the name of the paw!" I commanded. "I'm investigating a biscuit mystery on Foxie's terrier-tory. Tell me about the boys at the park this morning."

"We chased sticks. We saw holes,"

said a Squeke.

"We saw rabbits. We saw boys," said another.

"We…" began the third.

"Stop right there!" I jack-yapped. "Tell me about the boys."

Jack's Glossary

Jackie Wackie. *Auntie Tidge is the only person allowed to call me that.*

Interrier-gate. *Official questioning, done by a terrier.*

Jaw-dueling. *Loud, ferocious jaw-to-jaw combat. No damage is done.*

 The Biscuit Burrow

The Squekes had seen two boys at the park.

"They threw sticks," they said. "They kicked things. We chased them."

"Then what?" I asked. This *did* sound like Stick and Kick.

The Squekes didn't know. "Then we saw rabbits. Then we saw a big dog digging a biscuit burrow in the bushes," they said.

Biscuits again. This sounded promising. "What kind of big dog?" I asked.

The Squekes **con-furred**. "It was a *big* big dog. A *hairy* big dog. A *silly* big dog," they agreed.

I made an **inspired guess**. "Was it Lord Red?"

"Lord Red is a big, hairy, silly dog," agreed the Squekes.

Interrier-gating three witnesses at once was pawfully hard work.

I set off to Uptown House to interrier-gate Red. On the way, I decided to visit Shuffle. He lives with Walter Barkly, who had bought a roast chicken. If people were throwing food around, maybe Walter Barkly would throw the chicken.

Shuffle was lying on the porch with his jaw on his paws. He told me the chicken was hidden in the fridge.

Jack's Facts

People put roast chickens in the fridge.
Dogs are secretly working to learn how
to open a fridge.
One day, dogs will succeed and eat
roast chickens.
This is a fact.

While I was there, I interrier-gated
Shuffle about the biscuit burrow.

"What's a biscuit burrow?" Shuffle
wanted to know.

"The Squckes said Lord Red dug a
biscuit burrow in the park," I said. "I
sup-paws it must be a burrow full of
biscuits. I am on my way to interrier-
gate Red."

Shuffle got up. "I'll look for the

biscuit burrow."

"Report to me when you find it," I said. *"Don't* eat the evidence."

Shuffle went into the park. He was moving faster than usual.

I trotted across the bridge and up the hill. Before I reached Uptown House, I heard Caterina Smith calling. "Lordie, *Lordie*! Lordieeeeee!"

Jack's Facts

People do not call a dog who is at home.
Caterina Smith was calling Red.
Therefore, Red was not at home.
This is a fact.

I **pawsed** for thought. If Red was not at home, I would visit the biscuit burrow instead. I returned to the park. On the edge, I made a nose map.

Jack's map:

1. Shuffle the pug.

2. Chicken.

3. Lord Red.

4. A *whiff* of biscuit.

5. Boys.

6. *My own paw prints.*

7. Freshly dug earth.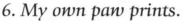

I followed my nose through the park until I discovered Lord Red. He was digging among some bushes. His paws were moving so fast the earth flew backwards over his tail. Shuffle was watching him.

"Stop, in the name of the paw!" I demanded.

Red pranced up to me. "Hello, Jack. Shuffle and I are detecting a biscuit burrow. Come and see, Jack."

"Are you digging up the biscuits you buried this morning?" I asked.

"I didn't bury biscuits," said Red. "Why would I bury biscuits? If I had biscuits, I would eat them."

"The Squekes said you dug a biscuit burrow," I **pawsisted**.

"I was digging *for* a biscuit burrow," said Red. "I detected it."

"You are contaminating a crime scene," I corrected.

Red stopped prancing. His tail drooped. "Am I really, Jack? I didn't mean to do that."

I applied my **super-sniffer** to the ground. Fresh earth, Red, biscuits… boys.

"What do you detect, Jack?" asked Red. "Do you detect biscuits?"

"I detect boys," I said. "I know these boys. I do believe I have cracked the case!"

Jack's Glossary

Con-furred. *Talked things over, done by furry dogs.*

Inspired guess. *A clever guess made by an intelligent dog detective.*

Sup-paws. *Like suppose, but for dogs.*

Pawsed. *Stopped to think with paw upraised.*

Pawsisted. *Kept doggedly on.*

Super-sniffer. *Jack's nose in super-tracking mode.*

Interrier-gation

The evidence seemed clear. I scented boys in the fog that morning. I whiffed them again where the biscuit package landed in Foxie's yard. I met them near Tina Boxer's shop. Here was the same scent again near the biscuit burrow.

In some ways, boys are like dogs. They like biscuits and sticks. They like mud and they run around.

"Boys dug this biscuit burrow," I announced.

"I know," said Red. He stuck his

rump in the air and sniffed hard at the burrow.

"Then why didn't you say so?" I asked.

Red scratched behind his ear. "I just did. Oh, now my ear is dirty. Caterina Smith will be cross with me."

I jack-jumped and gave him a nip. Red yelped. "Focus, Red," I snapped. "Describe these boys to me."

"They had sticks. They threw them for me. They poked them down holes. They kicked things. They buried biscuits. Then they saw me watching them and ran away."

"Let's get this straight," I said. "You saw the suspects bury biscuits in a burrow?"

"That's right," said Red.

"In this burrow here?" I was getting to the bottom of things.

"No," said Red.

Maybe I *wasn't* getting to the bottom of things.

"One of those other burrows. Maybe it was the one Shuffle is digging up right now," said Red.

I jack-jumped around. Shuffle was digging a new burrow. Or was he re-digging an old burrow? It was hard to be sure. Now that I looked, I saw five or six burrows scattered around. By the look of Red's paws, he had dug some of them himself.

"Stop!" I commanded Shuffle.

Shuffle stopped.

I peered into the burrow. It

smelled as if it used to belong to
rabbits. Red and Shuffle peered in too.
At the bottom of the burrow, I
detected some shiny paper. I sniff-
sniffed hard. Now I detected biscuits
inside the paper. They were unspecial
biscuits with jam and pink icing.

"Right," I said. "There has been so much digging already, we might as well finish it. Red, get over here."

Shuffle, Red and I began to dig. In less time than it takes Foxie to eat a sausage, we had dug up the evidence. It was a big package of biscuits.

Carefully, I dragged it out of the burrow.

"The boys left these biscuits for us to detect," barked Red. "This is a good game." He pounced on the package. His fangs went through the shiny paper, and a stronger smell of biscuit filled the air. I detected coconut.

A good detective asks questions about means, motive and opportunity.

I knew the means. Stick and Kick had buried biscuits in a biscuit burrow.

The motive was obvious. Boys are like dogs. They like to dig. They like to eat. Pawhaps they save food for later. They don't want anyone else to find the food. Or, maybe Red was right? Maybe they had left the biscuits for us to find? After all, they had thrown those biscuits in Foxie's terrier-tory.

The opportunity was easy. Stick and Kick had been at the park this morning. It must have been before I saw them at Tina Boxer's shop.

I knew all of this. What I didn't know was whether a crime had been committed.

It is not a crime to bury things, unless you do it in Auntie Tidge's vegetable patch. It's not a crime to feed dogs, unless you feed them **doggled** biscuits. So why had Stick and Kick run away when they saw me at the shop? Were they afraid I might detect their biscuits? Why hadn't they run to the park to guard their burrow? Did they *hope* I would detect their biscuits? Why hadn't they run to the park to watch me do it?

Jack's Glossary

Doggled. *Like nobbling a racehorse by doing something that will stop it from winning a race, but done to a dog. Also filled with sleeping medicine to quiet a dog.*

# Identity Check

At this stage of my deductions, I heard the sound of paper ripping.

Red had the evidence between his paws. He was peeling off the paper.

"Red!" I snapped. "What are you doing?"

"He's going to eat the biscuits," said Shuffle. He stuck his nose between Red's paws. "I want some too." He grabbed the other end of the package and pulled. The paper ripped and biscuits slithered out.

Red snapped up seven biscuits

and gulped them down. Shuffle
dragged the packet away, and Red
pounced on him. Shuffle bit Red's lip
and Red howled.

"Stop!" I jack-yapped.

They took no notice. Red trod on
Shuffle's nose and Shuffle sneezed
and growled. Red snapped up more

biscuits and swallowed them whole.

I jack-yapped again, then yelped as somebody bit my tail. "Gotcha!" snarled Foxie. I jack-jumped around. "What are you doing here?"

"I tracked you down," said Foxie. "And what do I find? You have biscuits! You said you didn't have any biscuits. You lied."

"I didn't have any then," I objected. "And I don't have them now. Red and Shuffle have them."

"Not for much longer," said Foxie. He darted under Red's belly and grabbed the biscuit package. It was half-empty and bits of it were scattered all around the burrow.

Foxie ran off through the bushes,

shedding bits of paper and biscuit.

Red and Shuffle went on growling and snuffling and rolling around.

I sidestepped them and sniff-sniffed around the burrow.

Right at the bottom was a corner of paper bag. I scrabbled at it with my paws until I could lift it out. It smelled strongly of licorice. I chewed through the bag and subjected the contents to **jaw-rensic testing**.

Next, I checked the burrow Red had been digging. At the bottom, I found a box that smelled of toffee, and another package of biscuits. I pulled them out and performed an **identity check**.

The first biscuit passed muster, so I tested another to be sure.

I was still performing identity checks when I heard a familiar voice. "Lordie, *Lordie*! Lordieeeeee!"

"Caterina Smith is calling," said Lord Red. He stopped scuffling with Shuffle and took off through the bushes.

I identity checked another biscuit. Shuffle snorted and wheezed as he jaw-rensic tested the licorice.

We were still busy when I heard Walter Barkly calling Shuffle. Next, I heard Sarge call me.

Time to go. I scooted through the bushes, jack-jumped into Sarge's arms and **greeted** him. Sarge frowned at me.

"What have you been up to, Jack? Why's your tongue black?"

<u>Jack's Facts</u>

Chow chows' tongues are black.
Other dogs' tongues are pink.
Jack Russells' tongues are black if
they've eaten licorice.
This is a fact.

I licked Sarge's face again, and left a smear.

Sarge sniffed. "Smells like licorice. Where did you get that?"

I was about to show Sarge the evidence when I remembered something. Sarge didn't know about the boys. He might take the mystery biscuits away. Thinking quickly, I **jack-knifed** out of his arms and set off for home. I was confident that he'd follow.

Jack's Glossary

Jaw-rensic testing. *Testing done by chewing.*

Identity check. *Usually performed by sniffing or biting.*

Greet. *This is done by rising to the hind legs and clutching a person with the paws while slurping them up the face.*

Jack-knife. *A kind of sudden leap and twist performed by Jacks when they want to get down in a hurry.*

 Under Arrest

Three hours later, we were all under arrest.

It was Foxie, Red and Shuffle's fault. Some dogs don't know when to cut their losses. Other dogs just can't hold their biscuits.

Sarge caught Foxie with the end of the biscuit package. I saw it happen. Sarge tried to get the package. Foxie snapped at Sarge, and Sarge chased him home.

Walter Barkly caught Shuffle

halfway through a licorice rope. I saw that happen too. Shuffle growled and pulled the licorice rope until it snapped.

Caterina Smith's carpet caught a horrible mess. The biscuits Red ate disagreed with him. I didn't see that happen, but I heard about it. Caterina Smith called Sarge and Auntie Tidge. She said she was taking Red to the vet, in case he'd been poisoned.

When Auntie Tidge heard that, she took Foxie and me to the vet. We all met up in the waiting room.

"Hello," Red said when he spotted Foxie and me. He didn't leap around. His nose looked dry. "I'm sick with poison biscuit. What if I die?"

"We're not speaking to you," growled Foxie.

"I'm really sick," said Red. "My belly hurts. My head hurts. My teeth hurt. My lip hurts. My ear hurts. Those biscuits were poisoned."

"**Dogwash**!" I said.

"Why do I hurt, then?"

"You had a fight with Shuffle," I reminded him. "He bit your lip. And I bit your ear, to make you pay attention."

"You didn't bite my belly," moaned Red. "The poison biscuits bit my belly."

"You ate too much," I said. "Foxie and Shuffle ate the same biscuits. So did I. We're not sick."

Just then, it was our turn to see
the vet. We didn't enjoy it.

The vet poked Foxie and me. He
looked in our ears and eyes. He stuck
things under our tails. He said we
looked fine, but that we should be
kept under observation.

"Dogs that wander around can eat all sorts of bad things," he said.

Auntie Tidge took us home. She called Dora Barkins and Gloria Smote and told them what the vet said. After that, half the dogs in Doggeroo were under arrest.

"It's for your own good, Jackie Wackie," said Auntie Tidge as she shut me and Foxie in the shed. "You've both been naughty boys. Fancy stealing biscuits! This time you were lucky, but next time it might be a different story."

I didn't feel lucky. It was boring in the shed. I chewed my **squeaker bone** for a while. After that there was nothing to do except listen to Foxie complain.

I decided to work on the case, although I still wasn't sure there was a case.

"Why would the biscuit boys run away from me?" I asked Foxie.

"They saw your ugly mug," snapped Foxie.

"Dogwash," I said. "They knew who I was. They didn't say 'that's a dog,' they said 'that's Sergeant Russell's dog'."

"Maybe they ran away from someone else," said Foxie. "Were there any **boneheads** around? Boneheads use terrier toothpicks. They probably eat boys for breakfast."

"They ran away from *me*," I pawsisted. Then I remembered something. "They ran away from me *twice*."

"Once would be enough for most boys," muttered Foxie. He scratched his ribs.

"The first time was when I first

detected the biscuits," I explained. "I was pawtrolling–er–" I stopped, because I'd remembered where I had been at the time.

"Don't mind me," growled Foxie. "You were pawtrolling the pawrimeter of *my* terrier-tory."

"Only because you were asleep," I said. "Otherwise you'd have been pawtrolling yourself." Foxie muttered at me then, but I pretended not to hear. "I detected biscuits and jack-yapped to tell the boys I wanted some. They threw the package over the fence and ran away."

Foxie's eyes gleamed. "They thought you were me," he said, "since you were in my terrier-tory and it was foggy. Therefore they were running away from *me*. It makes sense. It's a well-known fact that fox terriers are more to be feared than Jack Russells."

Jack's Facts

Jack Russells have facts.
Other dogs think they have facts.
What they really have are opinions.
Jack Russells' facts really are facts.
This is a fact.

"They knew who I was at the shop," I reminded.

Foxie wasn't listening. He was still **chasing his line of reasoning**. "It was really me they were running away from. Therefore, they thought it was me who wanted the biscuits," he said. "That means they threw the package of biscuits into my terrier-tory for me. And *that* means Auntie Tidge had no right to take them."

I knew there was a flaw in Foxie's reasoning somewhere.

Jack's Glossary

Dogwash. *Nonsense.*

Squeaker bone. *Item for exercising teeth. Not to be confused with a toy.*

Bonehead. *Large dog with more muscles than brains.*

Chasing his line of reasoning. *Dogs like to chase things.*

the Sprats

That night, Sarge made me sleep in
the kitchen. Next morning, he let me
out to do what dogs do. Then he
called me in again.

After a few minutes, I headed for
the **dog door**. It was jammed shut. I
prodded it with my nose a few times.
I scratched with my paw. I whined,
loudly.

"Stop that, Jack," said Sarge.

I did the **paw thing** to show him I
had important detective business
outside.

"You just came in," said Sarge. "I'll take you for a walk tomorrow. I have to see the Johnsons about some trouble at the kiosk."

I pricked up my ears. The Johnsons are Jill Russell's people. Jill Russell is **ace**. I did the paw thing again.

"Tomorrow," said Sarge.

Jacks are good at escaping from yards. Jacks jump over. Jacks burrow under. Jacks crawl through.

Jacks are not so good at escaping from a house. Houses have roofs. Houses have wooden floors. Houses have walls. Windows can be locked. Dog doors can be jammed. That's why I was still in the house the next day.

Sarge put on my leash after breakfast. Foxie was standing on a chair in Auntie Tidge's kitchen. I saw him banging on the window with his paws.

"Unfair! Unfair!" he yapped. "If Jack can go out, I can go out!"

He was still yapping as we headed along the street.

At the station, Jack Johnson bent to rub my ears. "Want to see the sprats, Jack?" He grinned at Sarge.

"Later, if we have time," said Sarge. "What's the problem with the kiosk?"

While Sarge and Jack Johnson talked, I made a nose map.

Jack's map:

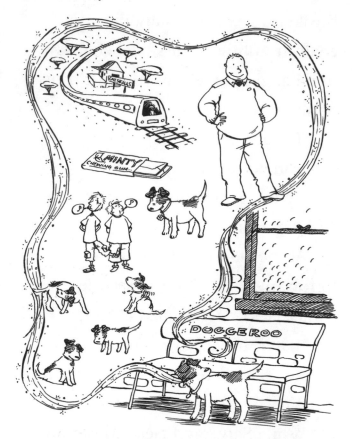

1. Trains.

2. Jack Johnson.

58

3. Chewing gum.

4. Jill Russell.

5. Boys.

6. Jill Russell.

7. Jill Russell.

8. Jill Russell.

9. Jill Russell.

What? I shook my head and **sneefled** to clear my nose. There was always plenty to smell at the station, but why was I smelling Jill Russell more than once? I sniff-sniffed again.

Surely my super-sniffer wasn't failing me? *Sniff-sniff.*

I couldn't work it out, so I concentrated on another scent. Boys. Sarge and Jack Johnson were heading for the kiosk, so I went too. I had my nose to the ground, because I knew that scent. It was Kick and Stick, the mysterious biscuit boys. I looked around, but couldn't see them.

"It's vandals," said Jack Johnson. "I could understand if they were hungry, but they just break them up and throw them around."

"Just biscuits?" asked Sarge.

"Toffee, chocolate, licorice, biscuits …all kinds of things," said Jack Johnson. "Just a few packages here and there, but it's annoying."

"Scattered around, you say?"

"Yes. There's no point to it."

"That might explain what the dogs have been eating," said Sarge. "Have you seen any strangers hanging around?"

Jack Johnson laughed. "Of course. It's a station."

Sarge laughed too. "I can't do much without any leads," he said. "If you do see anyone hanging around, give me a call."

Jack Johnson glanced at the clock. "There are no trains due for a while, so come and look at the sprats," he said.

Sarge and I followed him to the house next door to the station. I smelled Jill Russell again, and whined a greeting.

"In here," said Jack Johnson. He opened a door. Sarge and I went in.

Jill Russell was lying in her basket.
When she saw us, she got out and
poked me with her nose. Then she
went back to the basket. I followed
her, and looked in at a litter of pups.
They smelled like Jill Russell, but they
were hardly any bigger than rats. They
squeaked like rats too.

"That's the sprats, Jack," said Jack
Johnson. "What do you think?"

I sniff-sniffed carefully. Jill Russell
looked at me out of the corner of her

eye and muttered. "Watch it, Jack," she said. "Keep your nose to yourself."

Sarge bent down and peered into the basket. "Nice little pups, aren't they?" he said. "What do you think, Jack?"

I sniff-sniffed again, and wagged my tail. One of the pups squirmed over and tried to bite my nose. I felt my tail wagging harder.

<u>Jack's Facts</u>

Dogs wag tails.
Now and then, tails wag dogs.
This happens if a dog is especially pleased.
This is a fact.

Sarge laughed. "It seems that Jack approves of his sprats," he said. "Well…thanks for showing us. See you later."

Jack's Glossary

Dog door. *A door especially for dogs.*

Paw thing. *Up on hind legs, paws held together as if praying. Means pleased excitement.*

Ace. *Great, fine, the very best.*

Sneefle. *A snorting sneeze, done to clear the nose.*

A Bit Tied Up

It was ace to see the sprats, but I *had* to escape from Sarge to work on my case.

Foxie was under arrest. So were Polly, Shuffle and the Squekes. So was Red. Jill Russell was free, but she wouldn't leave the sprats.

What to do? What to do?

That's when Sarge got a call on his radio. He frowned. "There's some kind of trouble at Tina Boxer's shop. I have to rush. Could I leave Jack with you?"

"Of course," said Jack Johnson. He reached out for my leash.

"Thanks!" said Sarge. "I'll be back as soon as I can." He hurried off. I pulled towards Jill Russell, and whined. Then I did the paw thing.

"You're an old softy, Jack," said Jack Johnson. "Have another look, then I'll tie you up. I don't want you chasing Sarge."

Being tied up was not part of my plan. Neither was chasing Sarge. When Jack Johnson had gone, I leaned towards the basket.

"Get your nose away from my babies," snapped Jill Russell. She curled around the sprats.

I whined, in case Jack Johnson was listening. Then I interrier-gated Jill Russell.

"Have you seen two boys near the kiosk?"

"Don't be silly, Jack," said Jill Russell. "I've got sprats. Who cares about boys?"

"These boys smell of unspecial biscuits," I said doggedly.

Jill Russell snorted. "Most boys do."

"They kick things, and rattle sticks," I said.

"*Them.*" Jill Russell muttered. "*Rrrrrrrr.*"

"You saw them?"

"I *heard* them first," snapped Jill Russell. "They frightened the sprats. They made poor little Preacher cry." She nudged the boy pup with her nose.

"When was this?" I pawsisted.

"Yesterday," said Jill Russell. "They came kicking and rattling around while Jack Johnson was looking after a train. They were near the kiosk, but I chased them away." She muttered again. "They dropped some licorice."

"You are a **star witness**, Jill Russell," I said. "I should have come to you in the first place."

Jill Russell rolled the boy sprat on his back and started licking his tummy.

"Those boys are Stick and Kick," I said. "I believe they stole that licorice from the kiosk. I suspect they also stole biscuits and buried them in a burrow."

Jill Russell stared at me over the sprats. "You're barmy, Jack. People don't steal biscuits. They buy them in the shop."

"Not always, Jill Russell," I said. "Sometimes they steal them. We detectives understand these things. I must catch them in the act and deliver them to Sarge."

"Why?" asked Jill Russell. "Why should you care if boys steal unspecial biscuits, Jack? They're not special biscuits."

That gave me paws for thought. Maybe Jill was right. Why *should* I care?

"Stealing things is bad," I said. "When boys steal biscuits and bury them, bad things happen to dogs that dig them up." I told her about Red and our visit to the vet. Then I told her how we were all under arrest.

"That's easy," she said. "Just don't dig for biscuits."

"I won't," I said, "but how am I going to stop Foxie? You know what he's like about food. And Red won't stop. As soon as he forgets his bellyache, he'll be digging again. So will Shuffle."

Jill Russell said it was nothing to do with her.

"What about your sprats, then?" I asked. "Do you want *them* to dig up unspecial biscuits and get bellyaches?"

Jill Russell muttered. She had obviously changed her mind. "You'd better go, Jack. The quicker you solve this, the better."

"I'm a bit tied up at the moment," I pointed out.

Jill Russell climbed out of the basket and came over to me. She inspected me from head to tail. Then she put her paw on my head and pushed me down, just as if I'd been a sprat. "You'll have to pull out of your collar," she said. "That leash is too tough to bite through."

"I can't," I said. "It's too tight. And you know what happens to dogs that lose their collars."

"They get put in the pound," said Jill Russell. "Chin up, ears down, and *pullll!*"

Jack's Glossary

Star witness. *A witness who has good sense.*

 Pawformance

I did what Jill Russell said, and *pulllled*. I pulled until I thought my ears were coming off. I felt my collar slide up and up, then I jack-knifed. One of my ears popped free.

The collar slid over my nose and landed on the ground. It lay there looking empty. My neck felt funny without it.

"Hurry!" snapped Jill Russell.

I shook myself hard, then raced out the door. Some dogs might have tracked Sarge to Tina Boxer's shop. Instead, I scooted back toward the park. I didn't go in, but fixed myself a stakeout on the edge.

I made a thorough nose map.

Jack's map:

1. *Shuffle the pug.*

2. *Licorice.*

3. *Lord Red.*

4. *A whiff of biscuit, getting*
   stronger all the time.

5. *Boys.*

I sneefled and sniffed again. Yes,
boys. Stick and Kick were heading for
the park.

Boys are like dogs. They have
favorite places to hide things they
don't want found. They must have
stolen some biscuits from Tina
Boxer's shop.

Now I saw it all. They hadn't been hiding biscuits for dogs. They had hidden them for themselves. The package they threw in Foxie's yard must have been meant as a **jack-straction**. When I jack-yapped, they had thrown the biscuits to keep me from following them.

My stakeout soon paid off. Kick and Stick passed by me, heading for the burrows in the bushes. Their jackets were bulging with what my super-sniffer said were unspecial biscuits and chocolate frogs.

"We might need a new place," said Stick.

"Nah." Kick kicked a can. "Those dogs are all shut up now. We can camp out Friday night."

What could I do now? Some dog detectives might **pawform** an arrest, but Jack Russells aren't the biggest dogs in the world. I let the biscuit boys go past. Then I went back to the station for backup, and set up a **pawformance** for Jack Johnson.

I jack-yapped over and over. I growled and howled. I ran and yaffled. Jack Johnson rushed out of the station.

"Jack! How did you get loose? I told Sarge I'd look after you!"

I darted up to Jack Johnson and greeted him. Then I jack-knifed out of his arms and darted away again. Jack Johnson followed me. I almost let him catch me, but kept on jumping away. I trotted off towards the park.

Jack Johnson came running after

me. "Jack, Jack, come back!"

I tore past my stakeout and dove into the bushes with Jack Johnson chasing after. That's how he caught Stick and Kick red-handed, burying biscuits in the burrows.

Jack Johnson stopped trying to grab me. He grabbed Stick and Kick instead. Then he made them go back to the station. He **terrier-phoned** Sarge at Tina Boxer's shop, and Sarge came to take the biscuit boys into custody.

A couple of days later, Foxie said he saw them scrubbing the station kiosk. Ralf Boxer said they planted flowers around Tina Boxer's shop. Red said he saw them walking the Squekes. They were so busy they didn't have time to steal biscuits.

I didn't see any of that. I was too busy helping Jill Russell with the sprats. My pawformance had frightened them a bit. Not much, because Jack Russell sprats are the bravest pups around. "You're pawfectly ace," I told little Preacher, and he bit my nose.

Jack's Glossary

Jack-straction. *Distraction by a Jack OR an attempt to distract a Jack.*

Pawform. *Do, for dogs.*

Pawformance. *A splendid act put on by a talented dog.*

Terrier-phones. *Things that ring.*